Individual contributions are copyright © 2021 Jupiter Jones
Cover artwork copyright © 2021 Ad Hoc Fiction

Published by Ad Hoc Fiction.
www.AdHocFiction.com

All rights reserved. No part of this publication may be reproduced, distributed, or transmitted in any form or by any means, including photocopying, recording, or other electronic or mechanical methods, without the prior written permission of the publisher, except in the case of brief quotations embodied in critical reviews and certain other non-commercial uses permitted by copyright law. For permission requests, email the publisher, quoting 'Attention Permissions Coordinator' in the subject bar, at the address below:
permissions@adhocfiction.com

Purchasing Information:
Paperback available from www.AdHocFiction.com
E-book available from all usual outlets.

Printed in the United Kingdom.
First Printing 2021.

ISBN paperback 978-1-912095-98-8
ISBN e-Book 978-1-912095-37-7

This is a work of fiction. Names, characters, businesses, places, events and incidents are either the products of the author's imagination or used in a fictitious manner. Any resemblance to actual persons, living or dead, or actual events is purely coincidental.

The Death and Life of Mrs Parker

by

Jupiter Jones

For my friend, Ceri, who left the party much too early.

Contents

Prologue: On Time. 1

At The Oriental Dragon. 2
Feeling Most Peculiar. 5
Prime Ministers 8
Oh, You Sweet Boy. 9
Stayin' Alive. 11
Improper Introductions. 13
Pump 16
Pump Failure. 18
Starfish and Starfuckers. 21
Substance. 23
Oil and Water 25
Formidable Mrs Kite 27
Ten Things You Should Know About Bobby 30
Wasp. 34
Pemberley 37
Switch. 40
Corroders and Exploders 43

A Quickie 45
Legendary Brock MacBain 46
Sometimes Only Silence Will Do 50
George Redux 52
A Visit to Mrs Kite 54
Mrs Parker's Hit Parade 57
The Lover and the Loved 59
Another Visit to Mrs Kite 62
Day Trip to Southport 65
What they Argued About 68
Whoosh! 71
My Mother was a Tiller Girl 73
Like Bad Sex 75

About the Author 79
Acknowledgements 81

Prologue: On Time

A theory expounded by Heidegger is that time is a series of 'nows', each one always already the subject of a *flash* of experience, and all hurtling towards the finitude that defines our existence.

~~~

It is quite possible that time does not conform to the linear configuration we casually ascribe to it. Events, those notable notches on time's bedpost, may happen non-sequentially, casting shadows into our future, reaching backwards, rewiring our histories.

~~~

There may come a point, a crisis perhaps, when all those events, those flashes of instant now-ness, must, as Hamlet said, 'give us pause', or perhaps quite a jolt, when they become telescoped and fold into one another, a pocket-sized life. The End.

At The Oriental Dragon

2013

While we wait, you might as well know how the evening started. The ambulance will take thirteen minutes to arrive.

~~~

Bobby had booked the table for eight-thirty, but because of our argument, it's a whisker after nine when we arrive. The Oriental Dragon has a spicy fragrance, and a respectability that you don't always get with foreign food. Bobby says it's dated. I like its gilt-framed mirrors and glimmering tea lights which are flattering for mature skin. And proper starched linen on the tables; I would prefer white, but the linen is apricot. Best of all, I like the big fancy tropical fish tank, and right on cue, the fish all swim towards me, smiling, a shimmering rainbow of mollies and guppies, clownfish, angelfish, swordtails. Skulking at the bottom is a beautiful black ghost knifefish.

'Mrs Parker. Dear lady, a thousand welcomes.' Mr Lee comes right over as soon as he sees us. I swear he is shrinking, though he was never what you'd describe as tall, and his black suits are turning shabby, but he bows, that way they do, as charming as ever. He has the knack of intimacy.

'And Mr Bobby too. How ... splendid!'

I can hear Bobby grinding the porcelain veneer of his new crowns, and I smile at that delicious pause as Mr Lee searches for the *bon mot*, though he was born in Morecambe.

Yes, they have kept our table. No, Mr Lee lies, our lateness hasn't put them out in the slightest. The waiters come hovering like dragonflies with Campari soda for Bobby and my large gin. They know how I like it: very strong, very cold and no sliced fruit. I don't hold with turning good liquor into a fruit-salad jamboree.

The restaurant is chock-a-block with the usual Saturday-night crowd, animated with the sound of laughter, chatter, clink of glassware, clatter of cutlery – not many are sufficiently dexterous with chopsticks, but still, they look very pretty. Maybe because of that silly argument, I seem to have lost my appetite. Does the restaurant smell different? Slightly off – an undertone of greasy bile?

'You know, I don't feel so hungry, Bobby.'

'Oh, Aveline, really?'

'You order for me – just something light, perhaps only *dim sum*.'

'Well, you must promise to eat something, you naughty girl.' Bobby sighs indulgently.

Bobby is a good bit younger than me; sometimes people assume he's my nephew. People like Mr Gerrard the furrier, who we saw just the other day. 'Oh, Mrs P.,' said Mr Gerrard. 'Who is that lovely young man you have with you today? Is he perchance your nephew?' Mr Gerrard can be quite theatrical in his phrasing and Bobby glared sweetly, brushing imaginary fluff off his velvet sleeve.

'Good lord!' Bobby exclaims, staring intently across the crowded restaurant.

I follow the direction of his gaze.

'Is that your Mr Gerald? There. Over there with the fat lady.'

'Do you mean Gerrard? Mr Gerrard? No, no, he's somewhat older than that, with darker hair and grey wings brushed back from his temples.' I always think he looks like a jackdaw.

'Are you sure?'

When I look back, Bobby is smoothing his napkin. He pushes my drink towards me.

'Chin-chin,' he says.

Feeling Most Peculiar

2013

Watching condensation bead on the outside of my glass, I feel most peculiar, light and fizzy as a sherbet Dip-Dab. And my heart is racing, racing, breath shallow, giddy with nerves.

'Bobby, I don't feel so...'

He puts down the menu and eyes me with interest. He has lovely eyes, almost green, flecked with hazel or gold. But then I can't explain exactly how I feel because of the pain. A piece of broken glass is inexplicably lodged in my windpipe. I look down, expecting to see a jagged bit missing from the glass. Have I taken a bite and swallowed it? I don't hold with this trend for gin in a *copa de balon*: straight up, hi-ball is the correct glass, but Mr Lee's daughter is a moderniser. The glass is not broken.

My heart is pumping overtime, pushing against my ribs, protruding into my throat, choking me, and all my arteries are full and fat as slugs in the wet. Bobby is stroking my hand, murmuring, and the words mean nothing.

Nothing.

I watch his lips move and I know, in that instant, that my whole world with my darling Bobs is a delusion, a great big spun-sugar sham, and that I mean nothing to him, nothing at all. Oh, I am a stupid, stupid old woman, blinded by flattery and desperate to be loved. He wants rid of me. He must have put something in my drink. Slipped me a Micky Finn as we used to say.

Perhaps I faint, or black out, only for a moment, but I don't remember how I come to be lying awkwardly on the apricot flock banquette.

Mr Lee comes quickly and yet discreetly, and puts his hand on Bobby's shoulder.

'Is anything the matter, my friends?'

Bobby says, 'I think Aveline is having one of her flushes.'

'Why, dear lady you look most unwell.'

'She'll be fine in a moment.'

'A glass of water?'

But I can't speak. Or will not speak, and I clamp my lips. My heart is still expanding, it blocks my throat, and I'm afraid to open my mouth at all in case it blurts out like vomit. Imagine that, one's heart being squeezed up one's throat and then out of one's mouth.

Escaping past teeth and out into the room, glistening wetly like something at the butchers. Landing in one's lap, to be hastily covered with a napkin, removed in a stainless kidney dish, fed to the cat.

Mr Lee bows and hurries away to telephone for an ambulance.

Prime Ministers

2013

When people, old people, I suppose, have a funny turn or are confused, somebody will ask them, do you know where you are, dear? Do you know who the prime minister is?

Why? Or as Bobby would say, 'What the actual fuck?' Does it matter? The country's in a mess, always in a mess regardless of which political monkey has got his coat hung up on the back of the door at Number Ten.

However, just in case anybody thinks I am losing my grip, it's 2013. The prime minister is David Cameron. And I'm telling you now, I think I have been poisoned.

Oh, You Sweet Boy

2013

For hours, my engorged heart races like a greyhound – and they are ninety per cent muscle – but my lungs hang empty and shrivelled as vacated chrysalis husks. (Hmmm, mixed metaphors there, dearie, Mrs Kite would say, worse than mixed drinks if you ask me.)

Presently, Bobby props me up in his arms and pretends to help me take sips of cold water from a glass.

'Oh, you sweet, sweet boy,' I murmur.

I don't want him to know that I know what he has done. I will not give him the satisfaction, d'you see? All the times I have been in his arms, on and off the dance floor. Now he holds me like I am a dirty rag, like I disgust him, like I will make his fine, striped, Jermyn Street shirt smell of wee, and, regrettably, he will never be able to wear it again. He glares at me as if willing my heart to stop this very instant. And as he strokes my brow and checks his watch, I imagine him strolling down Lord Street, next week, or the week after; he will be shopping for yet another new watch, Rolex perhaps or a Breitling, and hand-made suits and a Jaguar motor car. He has good taste, I'll say that for the boy.

He is so beautiful. But that way his face clouds over when he is displeased spoils everything. His mouth curls up in a smile and the words on his lips tell me everything is fine, but the glowering dark of his brow belies it. *Then* he reminds me of Mr Parker, George, who was my second husband. He was another one for saying one thing and thinking quite another. Liked to get his own way, but not through confrontation. A manipulator. But without malice.

'More than one way of skinning a cat,' George would say.

Bobby would need the cat skinned for him. He would not wish to soil those beautifully manicured hands.

One of the dragonfly-waiters flutters up to say he can hear the sirens coming along the street.

Thirteen minutes.

Stayin' Alive

> *2010: The prime minister was Gordon Brown (and 1978 when the prime minister was James Callaghan)*

'Ha!' said Bobby, throwing down the newspaper. We were at the tennis club, sitting on the terrace drinking Pimm's on one of those days that looks like summer and feels like Arctic Roll. I loathe Pimm's – too sweet – and I was trying to catch the bartender's eye to fetch me a bourbon and a blanket.

'It says in the paper that old Pinkie Bartholomew collapsed last week at the fish counter in the market, and they kept his heart going to that tune by the Bee Gees. You know? That *Stayin' Alive* one.'

'Shouldn't have bothered,' I said. I loathed Pinkie. A jaded old hanger-on with wandering clammy hands.

'*Ah-Ah-Ah-Ah!* It's a hundred and four beats per minute, apparently.'

Javier the bartender winked at me as Bobby stuck one hand on his hip and the other in the air, jabbing diagonally, never actually leaving his seat, but in spirit he was under the glitterball in tight white trousers and Cuban heels. He's never been to Studio 54 in his life. Lordy, I don't think he ever even went to the Twisted Wheel or Wigan Casino. Oh, but he has all the moves.

'*Ah-Ah-Ah-Ah*. Perfect for heart thingy. Come on, Av. You're usually good with a pop quiz. What was the year? D'you remember?'

I remember a purple velvet midi dress, I remember driving an old Ford Capri in torrential rain, I remember the clinic, the smell of antiseptic. I couldn't be sure, so George insisted. Said he couldn't countenance etcetera. So I got rid, but it didn't mend anything. I should have lied or told him Brock was strictly back-door.

'*Ah-Ah-Ah-Ah*. Oh, come on, Av. What year would that be?'

'Before we met, my sweet,' I said.

Improper Introductions

2013   *1959: The prime minister*
                    was Harold Macmillan

One of the men in green uniform takes my hand.

'I'm Frank. I'm a paramedic,' he says. 'Can you tell me your name?'

'My husband was Frank,' I said. 'First husband.'

'But *your* name, lovie, can you tell me that?'

Of course I can. I know my own name. Never used to like it, my father's choice, a bit prissy I thought, or I used to think, but I've grown into it I suppose. I start to say it, but Aveline stays in the crust of my mouth.

Besides, he's very forward. To be on first-name terms so soon.

I wasn't properly introduced to my Frank, the Frank I married, either. We met at a dance; I wore a taffeta skirt in cerulean blue with two stiff petticoats, handkerchiefs folded into the cups of my brassiere, hair up in a comb. My friend Nora and I sipped cola through straws and pretended we weren't bothered. A tall, skinny boy in grey trousers crossed the endless parquet gulf as if it was a busy main road. He flushed, and mumbled, 'Yer wanna dance?'

I didn't: he had acne. But it turned out he was asking for his friend, a great dancer, but who could barely string two words. Nora married the boy with acne.

The paramedic is still waiting.

'Aveline Parker,' says Bobby, flashing those porcelain veneers in a perfunctory smile, his hand squeezing my shoulder in a proprietorial way. 'She's seventy-two. I'm sure it's nothing. I expect she's fine.'

Frank gives Bobby a curt nod that says, thanks mate – but shut up.

'Well, Aveline,' says Frank the paramedic, 'can you tell me how you're feeling?'

I felt amazing. Frank was a mover, lithe as a snake, a kisser, a groover. The lights spun, I breathed in Old Spice and Brylcreem. I was gossamer eddying, lifted by a zephyr and the twang of the band playing covers of Eddie, Hank, Slim, and Lonnie. His palms damp, my mouth dry. We went outside. His tongue between my pink-shimmer lips, hands exploring those two petticoats. Only afterwards I found out he was one of the Rimmers. That family had a bad name.

'Frank what?' I should have asked.

'Er, Johnston,' says the paramedic. 'Can you tell me, how's your breathing? Are you short of breath? Is your chest tight at all? Are you on any medication?'

He slid his hand inside my blouse. His hand was cool and heavy. Oh Lordy, please stop my heart banging against my ribs like that.

Pump

2013

'Aveline, you seem to have a problem with your heart.'
 I've always had problems with my heart, giving it away, getting it broken.
 'Are you allergic to aspirin?'
 Twice I've married for love. Head over heels.
 The paramedic squirts something into my mouth that tastes like … And he begins to cover me in stickers. Fly spray?
 The human heart is a clever, four-chambered pumping mechanism made of muscle. The heart has four non-return valves: aortic, pulmonic, mitral, and tricuspid. The heart is fickle.
 Sweetheart, soft heart, warm heart, love heart, heart throb. Buhdum, buhdum, buhdum, buhdum. That's the throb of a healthy heart. Only mine is pattering; a mouse scuttering over a drumskin. Faster. Faster than that.
 'Just take nice steady breaths for me, Aveline.'
 Now he's got me wired up, my heart making zig zags on a little screen. I think it's a lie detector.

Alright, I confess, twice, I used my head and married for money.

The human heart is a pump; a mystery; lasts a lifetime.

Four chambers: two atria, two ventricles. Fish, on the other hand, they only have one atrium and one ventricle. Cold blooded? Cold hands, warm heart – that's what Mrs Kite used to say. But she'd warm hers over the Parkray all the same. Chilblains in the winter. She was a martyr to them.

The Queen of Hearts, she made some tarts. Now we're getting to the heart of the matter. The Knave, that must be Bobby, the Knave of Hearts he stole those tarts. Oh, darling Bobs, what have you done? Now I'm going to die, and not for love, but for money.

The heart is a pump, nothing but a muscle, until it's…

Offal.

Pump Failure

2013 *1959: The prime minister was Harold Macmillan*

The neon guppies in the fish tank opened and close their mouths. They're singing, crooning an old Cole Porter number: *I've Got You Under my Skin*. Frank used to sing it. Not mine, Sinatra.

'Okay, Aveline,' says Frank. 'I'm just going to check you over, see if we can't make you a bit more comfortable. Can you tell me – whoops, there she goes! Brian we've got no pulse here, mate.'

I've got you.

In a heartbeat, a missing heartbeat, everything changes. In that moment of nothingness, I cease to be a person. Dispensing with their rather matey introductions, they get down to the business of manhandling my body, doing what they think expedient, to keep it alive. But scant regard for my dignity.

'Start CPR,' says Frank. 'I'll bag her.'

Bag me indeed.

Frank unbuttons my blouse. His fingers are very sure of themselves. A waiter scuttles crabwise dragging a tatty bamboo screen – a thoughtful gesture – to save the other diners from the sight of my satin petticoat, the crêpe skin of my décolleté. Beneath the petticoat I'm wearing a substantial longline brassiere, wide straps, full support. I am praying they won't have to cut it open. I would just die of shame.

Frank and Brian set to. But all the while, I'm thinking of *my* Frank, and his shagreen case of old seventy-eights, dance hall classics. Not real shagreen, couldn't afford that. Frank was my first husband, married in haste. I was seventeen. I used to have the tiniest waist; Frank could put his hands around it, well, nearly. By the time of the wedding, of course it was thicker. I had to have the dress let out and I didn't dare eat a thing. Oh, but we danced.

Out of choice, I never would have married into the Rimmer family, but Big Frank Rimmer said no son of his would shirk his responsibilities, so we were wed at the Town Hall on a cold day in March. With my mother in the wind, and Papa having washed his hands of me, Big Frank paid for the reception at the Imperial Hotel.

'Welcome to the family, Aveline.'

We had nowhere to live, of course, so as newlyweds, we moved in with Frank's parents, Big Frank and Mary. Me and my Frank had the attic room, Frank's younger brothers all bunked up in the back bedroom, and Grandma Molloy, who never spoke, in the boxroom.

'Carry her over the threshold then Frankieboy, don't be backward.'

'Oooh, love birds.'

'Kissy-kissy.'

On our wedding night I got cold feet, and didn't want to go to bed. I'd spent the day in white lace and my hymen had grown right back. I didn't want to do it there, under my in-law's roof, with all the Rimmers nudging and winking.

Mary yawned tactfully, 'Well, it's been a long day,' she said.

Big Frank tilted his chair back on its hind legs and looked at his watch in disbelief.

'Come on, Frank. You too, boys. Bed! Scram!'

The boys smirked.

'Oh,' said Big Frank, realisation dawning, and he winked and tapped the side of his big nose. He lumbered to his feet and punched my Frank on the shoulder. 'Go to it, my boy.'

My face was hot with shame.

Starfish and Starfuckers

1949: The prime minister was Clement Attlee

I floated and then plummeted, and my skin was clammy. I had never really thought about it before, about dying, but I was scared. Lying on that banquette, tracing the flock pattern with my fingers, I gazed across into the waters of the fish tank. I watched the clownfish, angelfish and the neon guppies swishing about amongst the startlingly bright green plastic aquatic plants. Would they be the last things I ever saw? And it seemed to me that I might be swimming with them. I opened and closed my lips; a stream of tiny air bubbles escaped and drifted skywards. I had shrunk to the size of a child, and I shrieked as the trailing fronds of seaweed brushed my thighs, and I was wearing a ruched bathing suit that hardly held the water at all.

I was inordinately proud of that bathing suit, very *à la mode*. Some poor unfortunate children, like my cousins, wore knitted costumes, which doesn't bear thinking about, or they swam in vest and pants, the littlest in the nuddy.

This town really was on the coast back then, and the Isle of Man Steam Packet sailed from the pier at high tide. Now of course, although the pier is still there, most days, beneath it there's just sand and sand, and litter, and illicit sex. Only occasionally a tide.

Back then, I found a starfish. I found it in a shallow pool left by the receding water, and without fear I picked the strange creature up and put it in my little bucket with some water and some sand in case it was hungry. My starfish was palest coral pink, with a texture like the intricate beadwork on an evening bag my mother had left behind. It didn't move. I sang to it to make it happy. Eventually, I took it to show my father, who was resting in a deckchair with a newspaper over his face. He had a *laissez fair* approach to parenting anyway but was quite probably hungover and dreaming of high-kicking Tiller Girls.

'Papa! See here! Starfish!'

He showed no interest. But neither did he offer prohibition.

I took my starfish home as a pet. After three days, the whole house stank of death.

Substance

2013 (mostly)

He has nice hands, I thought. Frank, the paramedic called Frank. Kind hands. Kinder than my Frank who was not good with words, but otherwise handy.

'You gave us a bit of a scare there, Aveline,' he said, looking not in the least bit perturbed.

'I used to be scared,' I said.

'Is that right?' said Frank.

'But I got over it. I flew a plane, once, you know.'

'Yer a lying bitch,' said the other Frank, the one I married.

I fingered my jaw, tasted the coppery tang, tongued my teeth.

'Aveline. Aveline. Stay with us, lovie, you're doing just fine.'

'Frank?'

'Right here, lovie, you're doing fine.'

What was that taste in my mouth? Frank patted my arm, and I closed my eyes.

Georgie Porgie, pudding and pie. Husband number two. He had soft hands, clever hands, pencil-squeezer hands. A manipulator. Never said it to my face but he liked to think he had rescued me. He never understood how bored I was in that big house with all that new furniture to dust. I was used to hard graft. Started at Oily Joe's on Winston Street when I was thirteen, scrubbing grease and ketchup off a thousand plates. Then running up and down the stairs at the Belle View. Up and down, making beds and scrubbing out bathtubs. Up and down, all bloody day, seven days a week in the season. Hard graft, that was. Then at Blundell's, the department store, gone now of course, converted into overpriced flats. Five-and-a-half days a week there, a luxury, apart from being in heels all day, and that hideous brown uniform. Five-and-a-half days of being nobody. That's graft too. A different kind of hard, but still graft. Not like squirting polish onto a duster.

'Hush, Aveline,' said Bobby.

I had my own business too, you know? After the divorce, second divorce, that is, I opened a shop in the arcade with the money they gave me to go away and keep my head down. Had to earn my own living again, do you see? A boutique really, *Fancy Pants*, sold Occasion Wear, I was quite the businesswoman in those days. Quite the businesswoman.

'Oh, God,' said Bobby, rolling his eyes. 'She thinks she's a woman of substance.'

Did I say any of that out loud?

Oil and Water

> *1955: The prime minister*
> *was Sir Anthony Eden*

'Six nights a week, start at five, no smoke-breaks, no whinging,' said Oily Joe, and I thought he was leering, so I crossed my arms over my little breastbuds. I was thirteen, and after a run-in with Papa, about taking responsibility for myself, which he said I should, and I didn't want to, but just to spite him I did, and I started work at Oily Joe's. Joe's belly spilled over his trousers and he scratched a lot. He did leer too but being boss-eyed you couldn't always know when.

Mostly, I was in the back, up to my elbows in the sink, hair tied in an elastic band, damp to my bellybutton from the suds. In a world of my own, humming, dreaming, oblivious to the chemical incompatibility of grease and soap as they fought for supremacy in the cooling water that swam with shoals of food particles. Rita, who was fifteen, helped out front, her skinny arms marked with welts from the hot fat. Kenny, same age as me, was in the yard, humping sacks of spuds, feeding them into the peeler.

The fryers there were a national disgrace.

'I clean them fryers out every week,' said Oily Joe. A bare-faced lie if ever there was one.

When they were occasionally emptied – of the congealed, stinking grease, burned bits, unidentifiable black crustaceans fossilised in the dank and gloomy depths of the tanks – it was a long night. Sometimes, if Joe's back was turned, me and Rita and Kenny would swipe a bottle of Sarsaparilla and share it, wiping goz off the neck of the bottle as we passed it quickly round the three of us. Sometimes, Joe'd take Ken out the back to show him his unmentionable parts, then me and Rita'd have to do all the grafting, and our hands'd be red-raw from scalding water and the Vim and the Brillo pads, our backs breaking, and the grease-sludge thick under our nails and in our hair.

'That's disgusting, that is,' said Rita. Kenny just shrugged, like it didn't really bother him, and helped himself to a gherkin.

Formidable Mrs Kite

> *1967: The prime minister
> was Harold Wilson
> (him in the Gannex raincoat)*

On the other side of the bamboo screen, life goes on. I had hoped for something more elegant than being bumped off, surrounded by people forking down egg fried rice.

'Come on, Aveline, I think you're a fighter. You're a fighter, aren't you, dearie?' said Brian, and I thought, do you know, he reminds me of Mrs Kite? She was the lady I rented a room from when I first went to Manchester to look for another husband after my Frank was killed falling off a church roof (don't ask).

I had her address out of an advertisement in *The Lady*. Sebastopol Terrace was a street of narrow, sooty houses, but the area was decent enough with paths swept and milk bottles rinsed. Number ninety-one. I knocked.

'Mrs Kite?'

'Who's asking?'

She stood on the step with her arms folded over her paisley-patterned cross-over apron and over her flat chest, over her stout heart and the calcified arteries that led to her liquid centre. Her practised eye roved over my luggage and the length of my skirt before she was satisfied that I was respectable enough. I hadn't mentioned the twins, left behind in Southport to be brought up by Aunty Kathleen.

'Married, you said?' Mrs Kite was not yet letting me through her door.

'Widowed is what I said.'

'The Good Lord moves in mysterious ways, dearie,' she said, somewhat cryptically.

I followed her down the narrow hallway and into a snug little room at the back, next to the kitchen. There was a small fire burning in the grate and a dark-red tasselled chenille cloth on the table. There, she laid out her terms and conditions, and pocketed my deposit and two weeks rent before the pan-faced look wore off her face. I didn't like her at first, but we became firm friends. Of course we did. Rum and black was her tipple. Rum and black. There was no Mr Kite. I took her second-best room, at the front on the first floor. The bathroom was down the corridor, with a separate privy outside next to the coal.

She came straight to the point; she was like that, straight talking.

'You'd do better in gloves,' she said when I told her about my new job in the corsetry department of Blundell & Browne's department store. 'Good foundation garments, they're not to be underestimated, but you won't meet many gentlemen there, dearie.'

Of course, she was right, so after work I would go dancing with some of the other shop mollies. The Palais, The Carnegie, The Casino. Stockings and dancing pumps, a little lippy, last bus home.

Ten Things You Should Know About Bobby

Brian steps back and Frank takes over, trying to force my poor broken heart to splutter into life. Bobby, on the other hand, Bobby is smoothing his hair, patting his pockets.

ONE:
Bobby is sometimes older than he admits to. If the subject of his age comes up, he gets that coy look on his face and I am reminded of Elizabeth Bennett being quizzed by Lady Catherine de Bourgh: 'Pray what *is* your age?' says the old trout. And that's the way it is with Bobby; he doesn't feel any obligation to own it, his age I mean. He's had some work done (not that he'd ever admit it). But look at his hairline. No, of course you can't, not with his hair brushed forward like that.

Two:
Bobby is a proper dandy, peacock, popinjay. Always immaculately dressed. He spends hours at the tailors, at the manicurist, getting tanned and waxed. Looking a Bobby-dazzler is a full-time job. Fortunately, he doesn't have anything else pressing to attend to.

Three:
Bobby claims to be able to play the piano, and swim to an Olympic standard.

Four:
Humble beginnings. Bobby used to work at Pontins. Not as a redcoat, although I'm sure he would have been exceptional. No, a chalet maid. Perhaps they have a different word for the boy-maids. Caretaker sounds like too much responsibility. Concierge is a rather Bobby word with a hint of eurotrash. Cleaner, scrubber, flunky. Yes, flunky, let's go with that. Flunky, until he was flunk out on his ear for rendering additional services for cash. When the woman said he wasn't worth the amount he charged and she would only pay by the inch, there was an exchange of insults.

'Porked with chipolata,' she said.
'Like humping old blancmange,' he said.

She sat on her purse and threatened to call the manager. Bobby swiped a pair of her earrings and threatened to tell her husband. It turned out the husband was hiding in the cupboard with his Super8. Gross Misconduct: Bringing the company into disrepute. Bobby doesn't like to talk about it.

Five:
Bobby is allergic to shellfish.

Six:
Bobby nearly died of peritonitis. In a dire emergency, Bobby had his appendix removed, by a drunken, struck-off surgeon, without general anaesthetic, on a cruise ship, or perhaps a private yacht, anchored off the coast of Malta, or Madeira, and afterwards, Princess Margaret helped nurse him. I have seen the scar, so some of this may be true.

Seven:
I first met Bobby on a train. I was travelling first-class and alone, feeling a little blue. The sliding door swooshed open and Bobby stuck his head in.

'Awfully sorry to trouble you, miss. Would you be at all put out if I were to join you at your table? There is an old groper next door, who has just … just…' and his voice dropped to a whisper, '…propositioned me. I scarcely feel safe.'

'Oh, you poor sweet boy!'

I was fifty-nine, he was thirty-two. He slithered in beside me, getting his feet under the table, so to speak.

EIGHT:
Bobby is touchy about financial matters. He spends money like water. Just when I get cross, he surprises me with a little gift. Money talks.

NINE:
Bobby has proposed twice.

TEN:
He is still waiting for an answer.

Wasp

*2012: The prime minister
was David Cameron
(hardly out of short trousers)*

Bobby is sick. He lies under a blanket, whining. I have taken him aspirin and Lemsip and cough linctus and Lucozade. I put on a caring voice:
  'Can you face anything to eat yet, Bobs? I'm sure you should eat. Don't they say, "feed a cold and starve a fever"?'
  'Who says?'
  'People, you know, people say these things?'
  'What do they know? Anyway, it's not a cold. I don't have a snivelling cold.'
  'There's smoked salmon in the fridge.'
  'How can I eat fucking salmon with toothache and agonising pains all down my neck?'
  'Well, an egg then?'
  'I don't want an egg. When is the doctor coming?'
  'You don't actually need a doctor, just rest, plenty of fluids; it's only a—'
  'You heartless bitch.'

He turns his face to the wall and lies rigid in his martyrdom. It was the same when he had that rash, when he sprained his ankle, trouble with his sinuses; even indigestion can be a major production. When he has the least little ailment, he is peevish.

I don't like to dwell on the age gap between us, but I make an effort to keep the years at bay. It's not just hair dye, eyebrow tinting, curve control underwear, skin serums, some dental work, a little nip and tuck here and there – that's only the half of it. It's a state of mind. Young at heart.

When I sit down, however weary my legs and my back, however gratefully I sink onto the plumped cushions of the chair, I must never emit that old-person noise, 'Ooofff!', as I sag with relief.

When I am short of breath, I keep it to cool my porridge.

When I am stiff and rheumaticky, my lips are sealed.

Bobby complains all the time. Precious about his health, he needs perpetual reassurance about his general wellbeing and the likelihood of his living a little longer.

'Aveline. Aaaaveline!'

'Yes, Bobby?'

'Don't leave me, I feel so dreadful.'

'I'm still here, do you want the radio on?'

'No, I don't want the fucking radio on, my head is pounding, simply pounding – you have no idea. You don't know what it's like to have such delicate health.'

'Oh, you poor sweet boy.'

He emits a number of small, pathetic noises to indicate that he is suffering, undergoing the agonies of chronic ill-health, that he is a brave little soldier.

'Aveline.'

'Yes, Bobby?'

'I think I might eat something though, just to keep my strength up,' he says in a small, feeble voice. 'Could you make me some soup?'

'Soup?'

'Yes, chicken soup. But not tinned. Chicken soup should be home-made, you know? For the soul.'

No, I couldn't make any pissing soup. I am not the domestic type. I don't believe I have ever cooked a chicken in my life. Who does he think I am? I may be old enough, well, on paper at least, but I am not his mother. I certainly won't spend my time staying home, playing nursemaid to a sick wasp.

Pemberley

*1969: The prime minister
was Harold Wilson*

Mrs Kite lived vicariously through her tenants: There was Miss Worthing and Miss Tanqueray, doomed to desiccated spinsterhood, having lost their beaux in the first war, the one they called the Great War. And Mr Boothby, who had a downstairs room, on account of his leg. Then there were the various 'gentlemen', the door-to-door men who stayed with Mrs Kite when they were in the district and took rooms on the top floor. Gerald, Victor, Bert, Clifford, Trevor. *She* was on first-name terms with them all, but she said none were to be sniffed at. Mrs Kite was an avid follower of the ups and downs of my search for a new husband.

'Come on then, dearie, let's hear all about him.' She poured me a small rum and black in a sherry glass. That was her tipple, rum and black. 'Is he a looker?'

George was not a looker.

'Well, he's not very tall,' I said. He was barely five-foot-five, with a round, sleepy moon of a face and pale, watery eyes, pale lashes. 'He's not the one for me,' I said. 'Though such a sweetie, helping me with my coat, insisting on paying my taxi fare home. But I shan't see him again.'

'Because he's short?'

'He wears lifts in his shoes.'

Mrs Kite snorted and a trickle of something dark came from her nose. She wiped it away with a hanky from up her sleeve.

'He has such soft, pudgy hands,' I said. 'He doesn't look like he's done a day's work in his whole life.' I liked a man to be a man, with man's hands, at least that way you can expect money coming into the house, even if those hands dished out a slap occasionally. My Frank was a man. God rest.

'What's his name again, dearie?' Mrs Kite had her back to me, ferreting in the sideboard drawer. I thought she was after her snuff, but instead, she produced a newspaper clipping. A row of stiffs in collars, The Chamber of Commerce, or some such, according to the caption.

'George.'

'George what, dearie?'

'Parker, I think.'

'George Parker?'

I nodded. She folded the paper and slid it in her apron pocket, swallowed back her rum and black, reached for my glass, knocked that back too.

'Fetch your coat,' she said. 'Your good one.'

She shrugged her old black Astrakhan on over the pinny, and without any explanation she whisked me out and along the road to the bus stop.

'Got any change, dearie?' She took my purse and selected two threepenny bits for the clippie.

I asked her where and she shrugged her birdy frame further into her coat and wore her closed-for-lunch face for about a dozen stops. When we were almost out of town and into the dull, flat countryside, she dinged the bell to stop the bus. We alighted, and arm in arm, we walked a little way. Fields one side, big houses the other. It was early November, and the air was tinged with the reek of damp leaves smouldering.

'Just a little bit further, just a little bit. There! There, do you see, dearie?'

Mrs Kite gestured triumphantly through some gates to a brand-new, pale stone, Palladian-style house. To be fair, it had exquisite symmetry.

So, I bought some flat shoes and, by and by, George bought a ring with a ruby the size of a pigeon's egg. We were married in church with all the razzle-dazzle, the first time, and Mrs Kite was my maid of honour, and then the second time around she was my witness at Bowden Registry Office, when George took me back, older, wiser, after the Brock MacBain debacle.

Switch

*1978: The prime minister
was James Callaghan*

Two days ago, the very sight of the pale, salmon-coloured paper, the smell of the newsprint, which to me was hot, sour and metallic, had been enough to make me retch. I took my tea almost black and my toast dry. George didn't seem to notice. Now, everything smells ordinary, the nausea has disappeared, the bloating and tenderness – pfft, gone. Again. George doesn't notice that either. George is like that. He either notices things or he doesn't, as if someone flicks a switch.

'MacBain seemed rather taken with you last night,' he said, all the while running a stubby finger down columns of incomprehensible figures, making computations, squirrelling away information.

'Well, he certainly spiced up the evening,' I said, which was true, and oh, Lordy, it had needed some spicing up. A Chamber of Commerce dinner of melon cocktail and overcooked beef. The great and good of the city in evening dress with a lingering whiff of mothballs – tedious, stuffy chaps and their tedious, stuffy wives. Only, one of the chaps had invited this Brock MacBain as his guest, no doubt trying to schmooze investment funding out of him; he's loaded, apparently, and flamboyant, and charming. A tonic.

'Be careful there, Aveline.'

'Oh but … I mean … What I mean to say is … Well, he was just being friendly.'

'So I noticed.'

'I don't think … Well, he's *not* the marrying kind,' I said, resorting to being cryptic because I certainly didn't want to use the word homosexual at the breakfast table, and I wasn't comfortable with the alternatives. But surely, he was, (a puff) for as they say, the good-looking ones always are. And nobody normal, no man, that is, could have been so knowledgeable about corsetry *and* opera?

'But you are,' said George. 'Married.'

'Pass the marmalade please, George, dear.'

George pushed the *Financial Times* out of the way, to make room for what he persisted in calling *The Manchester Guardian*, and I spread fine-cut marmalade, knowing I couldn't leave it there.

'Actually, George, that Brock MacBain has asked me, well not just me, a few of us actually, to the races next Saturday.'

'Aintree?'

'No, not Aintree. He's in a syndicate with a horse running up at Ayre.'

'Mmm, it's a pity it's too far then, just for the afternoon.'

'Actually, he has a plane, or so he says, at some airfield, just outside Ormskirk.'

'Woodvale, I suppose.'

'Well, somewhere over there.'

'A pilot, ha? What sort of bird does he fly?'

'Oh, I don't know. I didn't really take that much notice, a something-moth-something.'

George's brows interlaced; he shifted slightly, turned the page. 'De Havilland DH82 Tiger Moth,' he said.

George knows it's a two-seater. Like I said, a switch.

Corroders and Exploders

1978: The prime minister was James Callaghan

Frank and Brian are hard at it trying to fire me up as if I am an internal combustion engine with a flat battery, worn plugs, seized points, blocked carbs. How many minutes now? Have I still got time?

Well then, I have often thought that people could be divided into two types. There are those who are plotters and schemers, manipulators and strategists, like George. They overthink. They tie themselves up in knots with all the internal turmoil, and a canker eats away at them from the inside. They succumb to the big C in the end. Their overthinking is as corrosive as acid.

Then there are seat-of-the-pants people. Impulsive, all or nothing, people who hardly ever stop to think a thing through. Too busy living in the moment. Such hearts are pressure vessels; one day, one tiny fracture and they will blow.

Boom!

Brock was like that.

'Have you ever been to Venice?' he said.

I hadn't. I'd never been south of Cheshire before I met Brock.

'There's a restaurant there, well, little more than a bistro, no menu to speak of, just the catch of the day on a blackboard; jugs of *orto di Venezia*; the most perfect *cicchetti*. It's just round the corner from darling Peggy's.'

'Peggy?'

'Guggenheim. Tell you what, we'll go this afternoon.'

I laughed. Affectionately. Indulgently.

'Come on, get your skates on.'

He was serious?

'There's bound to be a scheduled flight from somewhere.' He swigged the last of his martini and held out my coat for me.

'What shall I tell George? What shall I pack?'

'No time for that. We'll go as we are; you can buy knickers and toothpaste at the airport. Come on.'

And we did. I wondered if I would get to meet the famous Peggy, but apparently, she had already exploded.

A Quickie

*1979: Who cares who
the prime minister is?*

Dearest Mrs Kite,

Don't be too mad at me, I've done it again! My decree absolute came through, and yesterday Brock and I were married at Gretna by special licence. At this precise moment, he is stowing suitcases in the boot of his car (an old Jenson Interceptor – can you believe it!) and we are off to France, then perhaps Switzerland! I couldn't be happier, honestly.

All my love, Aveline MacBain.

Legendary Brock MacBain

1979: The prime minister was James Callaghan

I should have known from the very instant I woke and saw him, standing naked at the narrow window, little more than a slit for arrows. He had that faraway look. Beyond the window was all the purple, grouse-infested moorland that should one day be his, the gloomy mountains, baleful monarchs in rain-sodden glens, and beyond that, islands where they ate puffins and if they spoke at all it was in Gaelic.

'Well, well,' he said.

Brock MacBain was gazing, not out across the inheritable moors, but down to the gravel below. Of course, I couldn't see what – or indeed who – he was grinning at.

After a three-month-long honeymoon touring France, Italy, Capri, Monaco, we had arrived back at this dismal family fortress in the early hours and gone straight to bed. And straight to sleep. The room was cold and un-aired because we were not expected, not exactly welcome. In fact, I was not welcome at all. His family thought me provincial, which I was, and *nouveau*, and ridiculously stupid. Perhaps these things were also true, but I was never after their money. I married Brock for love, I was head over heels; I thought at times my heart would burst with the enormity of my love for him. Brock was in love too, of course, but with the idea of love, with the game of eloping. What larks.

I tried to pull Brock back into bed, but he would have none of it. Sulkily, I rolled about between the musty velvet hangings adorned with rampant lions, but eventually I had to face the music and go down for breakfast. Of course there was oatmeal. I toyed with it under the beady eye of Ursula, my new mother-in-law, and Great-Aunt Elspeth who sported a quite credible white beard, something like a nanny goat.

'Are you expecting yet?' she bleated.

'No.'

'Speak up, gel.'

'No, I don't believe so.'

'Brock was a honeymoon baby, born within a twelvemonth of the nuptials, wasn't he so, Ursula?'

Ursula paused with her cup almost to her thin lips and, having nodded her assent with the merest inflection, she sipped her stewed tea.

'And his father before him,' continued the old goat. 'And all his forefathers. The MacBains have all been great begetters and have got on with the job. No shilly-shallying. And mostly boys. A few gels, but mostly boys.'

I thought she had finished, but no:

'Perhaps you are past your prime. Brock should have picked a filly.'

I was thirty-six and this was my third marriage.

A lace-capped drudge began clearing the table and I surrendered the tepid grey glue without regret.

Not bothering to find a coat – I should have taken a coat – I slipped out of the heavy studded door. The damn place was fortified as if they expected rival clans or reivers any day now. As I wandered, I realised I was being trailed by an arthritic-looking spaniel. Glad of the company, I waited for him each time he stopped to sniff. He tried repeatedly to cock his leg but failed to maintain balance and was reduced to squatting, peeing like a bitch beside the corners and downspouts of guttering already scent-marked by other more virile MacBain dogs.

I wandered through yards and peered into outbuildings, stables, cobwebbed greenhouses, and dilapidated storerooms until, rounding a corner, I came upon a smart new mews and gravelled forecourt.

There was a four-bay garage with chintz-windowed accommodation above. And there was Brock, leaning against the flank of a spanking-new Bentley Continental. It glinted with chrome grills and waxed and polished bodywork. Brock was flirting with his mother's new chauffer; a flame-haired Adonis, buffing with a chamois leather. They were sharing a cigarette, heads close together, laughing, till they looked up and saw me.

Sometimes Only Silence Will Do

1979: The prime minister was Margaret Thatcher

Dust motes. I turned my mind inwards, away from Frank, this immediate, busy and persistent Frank, and wandered through that flat in Cadogan Square. It was just a tiny flat, and on the shady side of the square: the first property I ever owned.

I let myself in, the key was warm in the palm of my hand and the lock was oiled and efficient. It was still partly furnished, pieces of their old and ugly heirloom furniture, shrouded. Like me. Parked out of sight and covered up. The freehold was my divorce settlement from the one and only, the legendary Brock MacBain. He was a card.

The air was stale. The clock on the mantlepiece said twenty past two and I wondered if that was just after an indigestible luncheon, or the maudlin time in the wee small hours. Brock could turn night into day. Any time was a cocktail hour with him. In the beginning, Brock was just so much *fun* to be with.

For three months we ran riot through France and Italy, then we spent another three being miserable.

Zzzzzzz, zzzzzz, zzzzzz.

I opened the shutters and there, on the windowsill, a bluebottle was upside down and struggling against a mass of gossamer threads. An iridescent hard case, hairy. Do insects have hearts? Apparently so, but nothing more than a rudimentary pipe: the dorsal vessel. This one is growing feeble. Trapped. Still waving.

Brock fell head over heels in love with his mother's chauffeur. Then, and too late, the family conceded that I was the lesser of two evils. Anyway, the MacBains were 'old money' and wanted to hush the whole thing up, so Brock and his boy were packed off abroad. Brock's brother had just been elected to parliament, so he was understandably keen to avoid a scandal. Not that I would have caused any trouble for Brock; I loved him. I love him still. But they wouldn't take the risk, do you see? You would have thought homosex was still illegal, the way they closed ranks. Bobby says anything goes these days.

Zzzzzzzzzz.

I looked around for something to squash it with. Not to put it out of its misery but to hush the irritating noise. In the end I took off my shoe and the velvety, dusty silence was delicious.

George Redux

1988: The prime minister was Margaret Thatcher

Quelle horreur. A 'Single-and-Mingle' event at a hotel on the promenade. A function room of mirrors, burly women with big hair and big shoulders, loud men giving it large. So-so wine. Not for me, darling.

After taking shelter behind a garish display of gladioli, I weaved my way through the throng, clutch bag firmly under my arm, slipped out, and headed for a quiet, wood-panelled wine bar. There was George, flipping through his Filofax.

'Fancy running into you,' I said. He didn't seem surprised.

He ordered me a G&T, plenty of ice, no lemon, kind of him to remember, and we fell into conversation as if it was the most natural thing in the world.

'The boutique is doing well, actually,' I lied. 'Just popped in for a quiet one, after such a hectic day, meeting friends later.'

He looked downcast. 'And you, George? What brings you to Southport?'

'Oh, some investment properties.' I knew he was lying. He had that tick; he would rub his chin, as if thinking of something else.

'So, you're well? You're looking well.' Another lie.

'Yes, fighting fit, never better,' he said.

Over in the corner, a woman with heavily lacquered hair poured her soul into a piano, crooning away, *sotto voce*, for so-much-an-hour, *lonely without you, lonely and blue.*

She looks like the lonely type, a lone lush. *I'm broken-hearted, lost without you.* Why are so many songs about the heart? She's got a glass of wine on the piano – not her first glass, I'll bet. *So sorry we parted, when you loved me true,* and I know she's got a point. I was a fool to care so little for the life I threw away.

'Aveline, let's pretend that never happened to us, that parting, and all the loneliness,' said George. 'Let's get back on track, living happily ever after. Marry me again?'

Just like that. So we repeated our vows, even the one I had broken first time around – the one about forsaking all others, though neither of us could be sure I wouldn't do it again. Also, I lied about richer and poorer; I wasn't up for that. I was mortgaged up to the hilt, maxed out, overdrawn, teetering really. George was a lifeline. 'In sickness and in health' was another lie. George had already been to see a private oncologist for a third opinion.

A Visit to Mrs Kite

> *2001: The prime minister*
> *was Tony Blair*
> *(not much of a socialist)*

They had parked her halfway down the garden under a sycamore. I'm rubbish with trees but I know sycamore. It's the one that gets black spots on the leaves.

'Mrs Kite. Dearest Mrs Kite.'

'Aveline! Such a surprise.'

I passed her the contraband – twenty Players – and she immediately sparked one up and sucked on it, the lines around her mouth contracting like a cat's arse.

'You're a good girl,' she said. 'Now tell me all your news. How's the shop doing? Are you well? How's your love life? You can't still be moping over short George; he's been dead yonks now.'

Vicarious Mrs Kite.

We sat there all afternoon, me on the slightly damp bench, her in her wheelchair, Dalek she called it, and I told her all about my long, hard-work days and solo TV dinners, and then, while returning from a meeting in London, how I had met someone.

'He's such a sweet boy. Do you know, I have quite the crush?'

'You be careful, dearie. Sounds to me like he's after your money.'

'Oh, Mrs Kite, he makes me feel alive again.'

'Do you remember Bobby Crush?' She lit another cigarette. 'He was on *Opportunity Knocks*; you know, with that dreadful man. Page-boy hairstyle and lace cuffs, Bobby Crush, that is, not the other one. Well, I shall think of your Bobby as being just like—' She broke off in a spasm of coughing, her bird-like frame convulsing, and she fumbled up her sleeve for a hanky to collect the gobbet of rusty phlegm that the coughing produced. '—Bobby Crush.' Then she laughed like a drain, and it was hard to distinguish between that and the coughing. When she was done, she stuck the cigarette back in place and, through the side of her mouth, continued. 'Does he play Chopin?'

Two carers in lilac tabards came with cups of tea and some Madeira cake.

'Mrs Kite!' exclaimed one of them. 'Have you been smoking? Again?'

She chortled. 'So what? They're my cancerous lungs and I'll die soon anyway.'

'Aren't you scared?' I asked.

'What? Of being dead? Well, it will be terribly sad of course, like missing a party you were looking forward to.'

'No, not of being dead, but of dying, of the verbiness of death?'

'Verb. A doing word. Hmmm, I suppose I would want to do it well, to be proficient.' She crumbled her slice of cake and threw it onto the grass. 'For the birdies.' She winked.

Mrs Parker's Hit Parade

1945: *I'm In Love with Two Sweethearts* – Issy Bonn

1949: *You're Breaking My Heart* – Ink Spots

1952: *Here in My Heart* – Al Martino

1953: *Young at Heart* – Frank Sinatra

1954: *Heartbeat* – Ruby Murray

1962: *Heartaches* – Patsy Cline

1964: *Anyone Who Had a Heart* – Cilla Black

1965: *Can't You Hear My Heart Beat?* – Goldie and the Gingerbreads

1966: *This Old Heart of Mine* – Isley Brothers

1967: *Something's Gotten Hold of My Heart* – Gene Pitney

1972: *Heart of Gold* – Neil Young

1976: *Don't Go Breaking My Heart* – Elton John and Kiki Dee

1978: *Closer to the Heart* – Rush

1979: *Heart of Glass* – Blondie

1982: *Achy Breaky Heart* – Billy Ray Cyrus

1984: *Shot Through the Heart* – Bon Jovi
1990: *Groove is in the Hear*t – Deee-Lite
1993: *Heart Attack and Vine* – Screamin' Jay Hawkins
2010: *Jar of Hearts* – Christina Perri
2013: *Heart Attack* – Demi Lovato

The Lover and the Loved

> *2011: The prime minister was that David Cameron*

Fish have bones. Relationships are never equal. Accept these things as true, get over them if you can. That's my advice.

'I've been thinking, Av,' Bobby said as he buttoned his shirt from the bottom up. 'I think we might get married. God forbid anything should ever happen to you – it would be more convenient if I were your next of kin.'

I paused. There I was, sitting on the edge of the bed with a stocking over my hand and draped down my forearm, checking it for runs. I could see my reflection in the mirror, I could see the look on my face. So I said, addressing the ten-denier sock-puppet, 'Well, I've had more romantic proposals in my time. Convenience. Hmm?'

Perhaps it's impossible to get them all out, the bones, those narrow translucent ones, sharp as needles. There's that moment, during a fish course when you notice a look of mild surprise in the eyes of your dinner companion, and the rest of their face hesitates as they try to avoid damage to the inside, fleshy parts of their mouth. You can imagine their predicament: now they have *discovered* the bone, they must surreptitiously rootle around for the offending sharp without seeming to be in difficulty, but they need a moment. A moment to extract the bone, discreetly.

Fish course! Get you, Aveline – you who were brought up on a diet of batter scraps from Oily Joe's chippy on the corner of Winston Street. You've come a long way. Get you!

'More regular, more elegant then,' said Bobby, appealing to my better nature. He leaves the top two buttons undone, checks the effect, sucking in his cheeks.

It's a wonder we don't eat the more spiny fish like shad under napkins as if they were ortolan. I've heard that the French think it is from God that we hide under there. Ridiculous! We hide from one another. That is the principle of shame. A stinking doubt about satisfaction.

Bobby sneezes as a shaft of afternoon light catches his cufflinks, placed side-by-side on the dressing table in readiness for the moment when I cross the room: he will hold out his wrists, I'll fasten the cufflinks for him and kiss his cologned cheek, but momentarily, I'm distracted, by the glint and the stray thought of my erstwhile mother-in-law, Ursula MacBain, or more specifically, her collection of fish kettles, ancient gleaming copper coffins for brown trout and char and salmon.

Bobby sways precariously as he steps into his slacks. I don't cook fish. Except of course the boil-in-the-bag variety, but I'm not sure that counts. I pull on my stocking, guiding it up over a bunion, a still-trim ankle, serviceable shin, an arthritic knee, and spreading my fingers slightly over a varicose vein bluing its way indirectly up my thigh. Bobby looks away.

'Look, Av, I can go down on one knee if that's what you want – not in these trousers, obviously. And we could browse the jewellers, tomorrow afternoon; you could pick something out.'

And I could pay for it too, obviously. But that's by-the-by. And yet? Is that not the nub of it? The finances, mine and his? He does have a point. His position is precarious. A lover. If I was sick or dying, if they said next of kin, if things needed signing?

'Oh, Bobby, you dear sweet boy, let me think about it.'

In this irregular relationship of ours, is he not the one who is safely nested? The loved. He still had his back to me, but I could see his face in the mirror, and I couldn't be sure if the fishbone was in my mouth or his.

Another Visit to Mrs Kite

2012: The prime minister was still David Cameron

The woman at the nursing home looked as if I'd caught her with her fingers in the till.

'Well, even so, I'd like to see her,' I said.

'Are you family?'

'No. Well, yes, family. I'm all she's got. Now.'

The woman fiddled with the spectacles that hung from those loops for the forgetful, and it was obvious that she didn't believe me, but I suppose she was used to it. Old ladies who had outlived all their kin. Left stranded by the years.

'Very well.'

She led me along a corridor, recently mopped with a pine disinfectant, opened a door, and stood aside to let me in.

Mrs Kite.

I was expecting her to have a sheet over her; I thought they always did that with the dead, cover them up so they can't stare at us. But the bedsheets were tucked beneath her chin. Her thin white hair was brushed back from her brow and her hands were on top of the pale-yellow damask counterpane, folded together over her flat chest as if she were an angel. As if. That made me smile. Her eyes were closed, but that didn't matter, she saw me anyway. She always did. I felt a rush of sweet cold air as decades hurtled past me and she was there on her doorstep, in Sebastopol Terrace that first time we met, with her arms folded across that flat bosom while she quizzed me on my circumstances.

'No kiddies?' she asked. And I think that was the first and only time I lied to her.

I pulled up a chair by her bedside and took her cold, papery, liver-spotted claw of a hand in mine.

'Oh, Mrs Kite.'

I sat a long while, and nobody disturbed us. I sat such a time that I began to wonder how long it would be before rigor mortis set in and stiffened up her arm. I stroked her hand and talked to her – all the usual stuff, how the sale of the shops had gone through without a hitch, the money was in the bank, and I was a lady of leisure. How Bobby had proposed again, and I was thinking about it. How I didn't want to think about it: I've been married enough for one lifetime, and I've outlived them all. How I came as soon as they rang but it was already too late.

The blinds were pulled down, but even so, a shaft of winter sunlight inched across the bed and across the floor, making her room a giant sundial. Before I left, I got the hipflask from my handbag, unscrewed the top and put the neck of the flask to her thin, cold lips.

Just enough to wet my whistle; don't mind if I do, dearie. I poured a little into her mouth, then wiped the flask with my hand and took a good long swig myself. Rum and black, always her tipple; rum and black. It trickled out of her mouth, down her cheek, staining the pillowslip.

'Thank you for everything, dearest Mrs Kite. Here's to you. And ta-ta.'

Ta-ta, dearie, you take care now.

Day Trip to Southport

*1971: The prime minister
was Ted Heath*

The train pulled alongside the platform; I felt leaden. This was a bad idea. I'd lied to George about where I was going, furtively packing the two small inadequate gifts into my handbag. As this was the end of the line, I had no choice but to get off the train. The old station was almost exactly as I remembered it, only quieter, with the ghost platforms for the discontinued northern lines now quite deserted. I bolted into the Ladies, fumbled in my purse for a penny; the door clanged shut behind me, what a nightmare. As I washed my hands, I studied my pale, speckled reflection in the dirty, speckled mirror. A little more lippy perhaps?

Chapel Street and Eastbank Street both look just the same: dirty and cold. June's, the florist, is still there on the Lord Street corner, and three doors up is the newsagent where Papa used to buy his newspaper, ten Woodbines, and a box of England's Glory. Sometimes, as a treat, he'd buy me a Walnut Whip. Even now, I can summon up the taste of the sweet fondant as I poke my tongue in, down to the bitter, woody dryness of the secret walnut. I hurry past; I won't turn up with chocolates. Such a cliché. Besides, I have brought something, late Christmas presents.

Head down and push on into the cold wind with my heels clicking on the worn pavements; patent leather Mary Janes, on pinkish-brown sandstone. Overhead, a lone gull wheels and calls. A bus is idling at the next bus stop, engine rumbling, exhaust belching fumes. I give a little skip-step; if I hurry just a little, I could make it. But no, I check my pace, I'm not in a hurry. I've been gone two years, seven months and twenty-four days. There is no rush. If they have forgotten me, the forgetting won't happen this afternoon, it has happened already. Do they love Aunty Kathleen? Do they call *her* Mummy now?

It takes me twenty minutes to walk it, and as I get to St Luke's my pace quickens and slows, quickens and slows. I turn the corner into the street, two streets up from where Frank and I lived – until he didn't. A little crescent of neat diminutive semis, bay windows, and pocket-sized front gardens. Nothing special, nothing grand, but somehow self-satisfied, a cut above the surrounding terraces. Kathleen certainly thinks so. She sent me a photograph she took of the twins standing outside, one in a checked summer dress the colours of Neapolitan ice cream, one in an itchy jumper with a yacht on the front. Her with goosebumps, him scratching at his neck.

The house looks closed and smug. I think there is no one home, but I steel myself and ring the bell anyway. The sound is shrill and vulgar. After an anxious wait, I step up to the bay and peer in. No lights are on, but I can see into the front room, even through the net curtains, see the winged armchairs with their crocheted antimacassars, the clusters of occasional tables, and the paper chains drooping across the ceiling. I stand for a long time with my forehead against the cold windowpane. I had not imagined it would be like this. I don't know if I am too late or too early. Perhaps I should have written first. Perhaps.

I left what I had brought on the doorstep. *A Boy's Own Handbook*, and the Ladybird book of *Things to Make and Do*. What was I thinking?

What they Argued About

2013

'A trust fund? What the actual fuck?' Bobby said.

'Bobby! No need for the language.'

'Sorry, sorry, but after all these years?'

'They are still my kiddies.'

'When did you last see them? Hear from them, even?'

'That's hardly the point. They were babies when I left. Not that I had much choice. But still. I want to make it up to them.'

'They'll be middle-aged now. It would be like giving money away to perfect strangers.'

'Flesh and blood, Bobby.'

'Strangers.'

'Estranged maybe.'

He shook his head, like I'd suggested bequeathing it all to a donkey sanctuary. Perhaps I should have left it there. But it is my money. Oh, he spends it like water, but it's mine. Well it's mine at the moment. Once, it was George Parker's money, made off the backs of the working classes of Manchester. Polished up by the vanity of the middle classes until he had almost as much money as some of the old-money families. He said to me, George, that is, he said,

'Do you know what defines the upper classes? Do you, Aveline?'

I knew a rhetorical question by then. That's one you know the answer to, but you keep it buttoned, because it's not your turn to shine.

'They don't buy any new furniture! All their old stuff, mouldering for generations, it's all riddled with woodworm. None of that for us, Aveline. It will be all brand spanking new for us. Brand spanking!'

George aspired to join the uppers in everything except hand-me-downs.

He also admired the long game of come-uppers like the Salts and the Levers. George played the philanthropist, well, dabbled, but really, he was a squirrel – small, like a squirrel. Now, what's left is my money. Begins at home, I say.

'Maybe it's not too late. To mend fences.'

'Well, I wouldn't bother, if I were you,' said Bobby. 'Sleeping dogs lie, and all.'

I hate arguing about money, but I also resent his sense of entitlement. A man should make his own way in the world. So, I said – and this was particularly cruel – I said, 'And then, there's my grand-kiddies, there are five of them I think, and they're blood too. Blood, Bobby, its thicker than gin, you know?'

'It may be thick, my dear, but you can't just buy it back.' His lips curled in a snarl, he flung down *Variety*, and shot me a look of such utter contempt.

Still, that ugly moment was quickly over, and he seemed to see my point of view because then he said, 'Well, my dear, you must do whatever you see fit with the Parker fortune.'

It's not a fortune, but what's left is enough. I should have told Bobby I loved him, told him he'd be taken care of, provided for, and he will need it, when he's old and all alone like poor Mrs Kite. But just then, to change the subject, he checked his watch.

'Don't forget I've booked a table at the Geriatric Dragon,' he said. 'Are you getting ready soon?'

It was a new watch. Another new watch.

Whoosh!

2013

Brian stopped mashing my poor ribs to smithereens for a moment, and Frank put his cool fingers on my throat, but it was no use. My ticker had stopped. He shook his head.

'That's eleven minutes with no output, Bri.'

'Give her a shot then, is it?'

Mr Lee wrung his hands, and I noticed the cuffs of his jacket were frayed. The jacket was old with that rusty look that black cloth gets over time. He was as jaded as his restaurant with its apricot flock worn flat. Maybe business was not so good. Maybe time he retired, handed it on to his spiteful daughter.

My Bobby, on the other hand, looked quite *insouciant*. While Frank readied his syringe, Bobby attended to a speck of something on his velvet cuff.

And whoosh! My veins are dancing, zinging with adrenaline, which is amazing and makes cocaine feel like baking powder (oh yes, I've tried most things in my time). I feel I could easily jump up and tap dance on the tables.

I'm on a zip-wire with my knickers on show, I'm tobogganing down the Cresta Run, swigging champagne from the bottle, ice-cold air stinging my cheeks, I'm racing, racing, racing. And I'm twelve and I'm at the fairground, on the Waltzers and a gypsy boy with a money belt and a golden earing is spinning me round and promising to meet me afterwards for a kiss. And then I'm five and upside down with Papa holding my ankles as he whirls me round and round. Then I grow up again, older and taller, tall as trees, striding over rooftops, and I can see myself through a telescope, kaleidoscope, zoetrope. I'm in a car, an old rust-bucket, practising for the world land-speed record – or so Frank says – on the flats of Southport beach. Frank is drunk as a skunk, he's accelerating, faster and faster, foot to the floor, me shrieking for him to slow down, but the wind whips away my words, and he's laughing at me, and still laughing as the car flips and flies, corkscrewing through the night, still laughing as the car rolls over and over and we are both thrown clear just before it bursts into flames. Whoof! And the darkening skies are speckled with firefly-sparks. I have sand and salt in my mouth, I slap him, and he laughs, and he kisses me.

But my body, you see, that was still slumped like an old mattress.

My Mother was a Tiller Girl

1945: The prime minister was Winston Churchill

I don't remember my mother. I mean, I don't remember what she looked like, but I remember her scent. I remember breathing her in as she leaned over me, the powdered curve of her cheek. I recall the feel of *crêpe de chine*, the swish of a hem, the click of her heels.

She flitted off when I was three. My papa cried, but not for long. He was starstruck, a proper stage-door Johnnie, mooning about after whole chorus lines of hoofers, and bit-part actresses. The travelling sort, from threadbare theatre companies that toured the north west, 'Oh, I'm in *Rep*, darling,' they'd titter, but often, they were just the totty in an end-of-the-pier show, or a magician's assistants. None of them were interested in a ready-made family, in settling down to raise some other woman's brat.

So Papa brought me up, singlehanded mostly, but he was a dreamer; his approach to parenting was lackadaisical – benign neglect they call it now. I don't throw stones. What did I do for my kiddies? Left them with Aunty Kathleen and forgot to go back for them.

I wonder sometimes – who did they pretend their mother was?

Like Bad Sex

2013

Frank's hands are on my breastbone; thrust and thrust and thrust. He's on top and putting everything into that pump action, breathing hard, sweating. His hair falls damply forward over his brow; he smells of coffee, cologne, surgical spirit.

Beneath him I'm a plank.

I'm listening to the urgent rhythmical creak of those old bedsprings, and I'm holding my breath, hoping Frank's parents in the room below can't hear us. For the shame of it, I just cling to the bedshroud, a fold of it crushed in my hand.

And Frank's pumping.

At it, hammer and tongs, he is.

The muscles in his arms are rigid, but they're beginning to tremble, to give out. Every so often he emits a sort of snuffling grunt of exertion. Is he even close? Something is slipping away. Further away. I shut my eyes. It's like bad sex; impersonal and unproductive, exhausting for both of us. I shall be glad when it's over.

This Frank takes a breather. Brian pauses in his endeavour to inflate me as if I am a small dingy. He checks for a pulse and checks the time again on one of those upside-down watches pinned to the front of his uniform.

'That's twenty-two minutes, mate,' he says in a low voice. 'Still no output.'

Frank and Brian exchange practised glances. Mr Lee dabs his eyes with a napkin.

Brian shakes his head. Frank sighs and makes me decent. And they both stand up to offer Bobby their condolences.

THE DEATH AND LIFE OF MRS PARKER

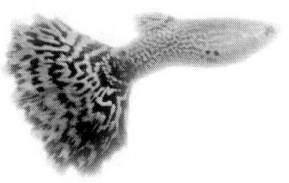

author photo by Nancy Davies

About the Author

Jupiter Jones grew up on the north-west coasts of Cumberland and Lancashire. The first was wild and secretive, the second trashy and jaded; she loved them both and they haunt her work. Following a brief spell in London to complete a PhD in Spectatorial Embarrassment at Goldsmiths, she now lives in Wales, and writes short and flash fictions. She is the winner of the Colm Tóibín International Prize, and her work has been published by Aesthetica, Brittle Star, Fish, Reflex, Scottish Arts Trust, and rejected by many, many others.

Acknowledgements

'The Lover and the Loved' (2021) was first published by Reflex Fiction [Online] https://www.reflexfiction.com/author/jupiter-jones/

I would like to thank Jude Higgins and all the Bath Flash Fiction team for continuing to champion the form of Novella-in-Flash. Thanks also to the competition judge, author Michelle Elvy for her kind comments. And yet more thanks to John at Ad Hoc Fiction, Johanna Robinson for fixing my punctuation, David Rhymes for all the encouragement, Joanne Reardon and Jane Elmor at the Open University for their unstinting generosity, all the A803 cohort, especially Maya Jordan for her answers on a postcard, and finally, to the Coven for their withering comments and endless snark.